Previously published as *Da Deng Long* by Beijing POPLAR Culture Project Co., Ltd. in 2017.
Translated from Simplified Chinese by Helen Wang. First published in English by
Amazon Crossing Kids in collaboration with Amazon Crossing in 2021.

Published by Amazon Crossing Kids, New York, in collaboration with Amazon Crossing

www.apub.com

Amazon, Amazon Crossing, and all related logos are trademarks of
Amazon.com, Inc., or its affiliates.

ISBN-13: 9781542029841 (hardcover)
ISBN-10: 1542029848 (hardcover)

The illustrations are painted in gouache.

Book design by AndWorld Design
Printed in China

First Edition
10 9 8 7 6 5 4 3 2 1

amazon crossing kids

PLAYING WITH LANTERNS

by Wang Yage

illustrated by Zhu Chengliang

translated by Helen Wang

There was always snow at
NEW YEAR in the north. When it
snowed at dusk, and on through the
night, and winter was at its coldest,
we would wake in the morning
to a new white world outside!

We spent the first day of the new year at home. From the second day of New Year, everyone went out, crunching through the snow on the ridges between the fields, to visit family and friends and wish them Happy New Year.

On the third day, uncles started giving LANTERNS.

By the fifth day, New Year didn't feel quite so new anymore. ZHAO DI couldn't wait for Uncle to come. He gave her two lanterns, as he did every New Year.

She had to be careful when she walked through the snow with her lantern in case she slipped or the candle blew out in the wind.

The sky was as dark and deep
as the sea. Lanterns near and far bobbed
like lamps on fishing boats.

"Zhao Di! COME AND JOIN US!"

Zhao Di and her friends showed one another their lanterns.

They were all different:
a colorful ACCORDION lantern,
a lovely PINK LOTUS lantern,
a STRIPY WATERMELON lantern,
and a BRIGHT RED GLOBE lantern.
Four beautiful lanterns!

Zhao Di and her friends walked around the village, their lanterns raised.

When a sudden gust of wind blew, they had to swerve quickly to protect their lanterns. The candle flames bowed sideways for a moment before righting themselves.

But Zhao Di's CANDLE WENT OUT.

Zhao Di's friends gathered round to block out the wind while she relit her candle from another lantern.

They saw lanterns bobbing at
the end of the lane and started
walking toward them. But when
they heard boys' voices, they
stopped, ready to turn back.

The boys raised their lanterns even higher. Then, all of a sudden, they **CHARGED** at the girls, swinging their lanterns at Zhao Di and her friends. When the girls squealed, the boys ran off, laughing.

The night grew colder and colder.
The village was quiet. Not a single dog barked.
"Our candles will go out soon," said one of her friends.
Zhao Di stopped to check the dim light in her lantern.

"Zhao Di, it's late! It's time to come home!"
Zhao Di's mother sounded impatient.

The other girls hurried home too.
"Let's meet earlier tomorrow!" said Zhao Di.

In no time at all it was the fifteenth day. Zhao Di woke to the sound of fireworks CRACKING and POPPING.

But the fireworks weren't as loud and exciting as those on New Year's Day.

They sounded sad, as though saying, *The New Year celebrations are over!* All day long, no matter what she was doing, Zhao Di felt empty inside.

It was the **LAST EVENING** for lanterns.
At sundown, Zhao Di lit her lantern and went outside.

Lanterns and laughter floated down the dark lanes of the village.
The smell of gunpowder hung in the air.

"Zhao Di! Come and make a circle with us!" her friend called.

The girls put their lanterns together and ran around in a circle, singing:

"GLOW, LANTERNS, GLOW, OR TO BED WE MUST GO."

The moon rose slowly in the sky. Zhao Di and her
friends grew tired of running around in a circle.
They put their lanterns down in the middle.

"SMASH THE LANTERNS!
SMASH THE LANTERNS!"
someone shouted nearby. At the far end of the lane,
lanterns were being swung and smashed together.

"Do we have to smash them already?" asked Zhao Di.

But she knew that the candles would go out soon and they had to smash the lanterns before that happened or it would bring bad luck. She didn't want Uncle to have sore red eyes again.

One of her friends started smashing her lantern; then they all joined in, laughing and shouting.

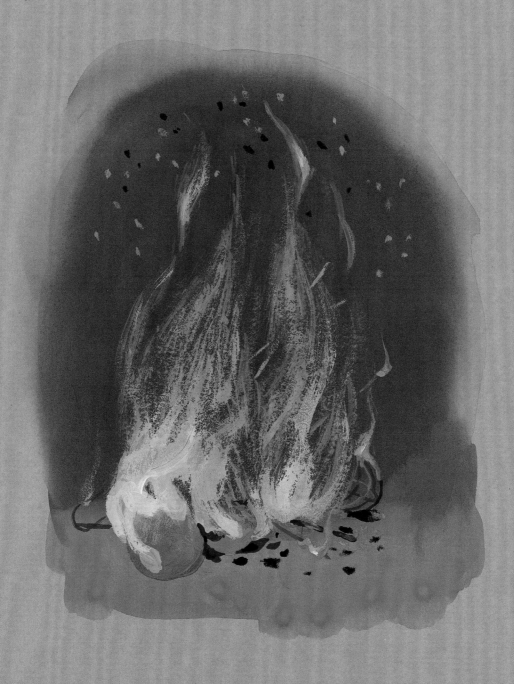

The lanterns caught FIRE. Zhao Di and her friends went quiet. Zhao Di watched as the tongues of the flames gradually burned the lanterns into a black hole.

The next evening, everything was quiet outside,
and Zhao Di lay on her warm platform bed.
She felt something was missing.

The New Year celebrations were over. She wished it could be New Year all the time. **HAPPY MEMORIES** of playing with her lantern floated before her.

Through teary eyes, she saw her accordion lantern LIGHT UP again.
Its soft, round glow filled her heart. She remembered feeling sad on the
fifteenth day last year.

"But New Year came again, didn't it? And there will be another New Year
NEXT YEAR!" she told herself.

A smile curled from the corner of her mouth and, thinking about the glowing
lantern, she drifted off to sleep.

Author's Note

"SMASHING LANTERNS" is a folk tradition of Shaanxi province, in northwest China. It can be traced back to the Han Dynasty (202 BCE–220 CE), when lanterns were burned to mark the last day of the New Year celebrations.

On the third day of New Year, people start to make gifts of lanterns. The main types are the bright red palace lanterns ("fire-globe lanterns") and accordion lanterns ("cowpat lanterns"). The custom is for uncles to give lanterns to their nieces and nephews— usually a pair of lanterns and ten candles every year for twelve years. In the evenings, each child takes a lantern outside to have fun with their friends until the fifteenth day of New Year.

The fifteenth day is the last day of New Year, and the custom is to destroy the lanterns because the festival is over. When the children finish playing with their lanterns, they must smash them and burn them, so they can't be used again. It is considered bad luck to save lanterns for next year, because this would make their uncles' eyes red and sore from pink eye!